The Man in the Iron Mask

Retold from the Alexandre Dumas
original by Oliver Ho

Illustrated by Troy Howell

STERLING

New York / London
www.sterlingpublishing.com/kids

STERLING and the distinctive Sterling logo
are registered trademarks of Sterling Publishing Co., Inc.

Library of Congress Cataloging-in-Publication Data

Ho, Oliver.
  The man in the iron mask / retold from the Alexandre Dumas original;
abridged by Oliver Ho; afterword by Arthur Pober; illustrated by Troy Howell.
    p. cm. — (Classic starts)
  Summary: An abridged version of the tale of the four Musketeers' final adventure during which they plot to replace King Louis XIV of France with the mys-
terious, masked prisoner in the Bastille believed to be Louis' falsely imprisoned
twin brother and the true king.
  ISBN-13: 978-1-4027-4579-9
  ISBN-10: 1-4027-4579-6
  1. Man in the Iron Mask—Juvenile fiction. 2. France—History—Louis XIV,
1643–1715—Juvenile fiction. [1. Man in the Iron Mask—Fiction. 2. France—
History—Louis XIV, 1643–1715—Fiction. 3. Prisoners—Fiction. 4. Brothers—
Fiction. 5. Twins—Fiction. 6. Adventure and adventurers—Fiction.] I. Howell,
Troy, ill. II. Dumas, Alexandre, 1802–1870. Homme au masque de fer. English.
III. Title.

PZ7.H63337Man 2008
[Fic]—dc22
                                                                    2007009221

2 4 6 8 10 9 7 5 3 1

Published by Sterling Publishing Co., Inc.
387 Park Avenue South, New York, NY 10016
Copyright © 2008 by Oliver Ho
Illustrations copyright © 2008 by Troy Howell
Distributed in Canada by Sterling Publishing
ᶜ/ₒ Canadian Manda Group, 165 Dufferin Street,
Toronto, Ontario, Canada M6K 3H6
Distributed in the United Kingdom by GMC Distribution Services,
Castle Place, 166 High Street, Lewes, East Sussex, England BN7 1XU
Distributed in Australia by Capricorn Link (Australia) Pty. Ltd.
P.O. Box 704, Windsor, NSW 2756, Australia

Classic Starts is a trademark of Sterling Publishing Co., Inc.

Printed in China
All rights reserved

Sterling ISBN-13: 978-1-4027-4579-9
ISBN-10: 1-4027-4579-6

For information about custom editions, special sales, premium and
corporate purchases, please contact Sterling Special Sales
Department at 800-805-5489 or specialsales@sterlingpublishing.com.

CONTENTS

❧

CHAPTER 1

Aramis and the Prisoner

Aramis arrived at the Bastille late. It was the most infamous prison in France, and he was there to see one of its prisoners.

"I will speak to him alone," Aramis said.

He took the guard's lantern and stepped inside the prisoner's cell. Then he signaled for the guard to close the door. Beneath the cell's one small window, a young man was lying on a bed. His face was half hidden by his arms. Aramis sat on a chair next to the bed, and the young man lifted his head.

"What do you want of me?" the prisoner asked in a cold, strong voice.

"I want you to think back to your childhood," Aramis said. "Do you remember a man who used to visit and a lady who wore black silk and had fiery ribbons in her hair?"

"Yes," said the young man thoughtfully. "I asked once who that man was, and my nurse told me that he was a priest. I remember being surprised by how much he looked like a soldier. When I questioned my nurse about it, she said that he had once been a great Musketeer. She told me the Musketeers were the best soldiers in France, dedicated to protecting the King." The young man looked up. "It's you. I recognize you now. You're the man who used to visit me."

Aramis nodded. "I am now a bishop in the church," he said, "and I have risked everything to find you. If the king learned of this meeting between us tonight, tomorrow I would see the depths of a dungeon far darker than this cell. Fortunately, he doesn't know of your existence, but there are others who do, and they might inform him."

Listening to these sharp words, the young man sat up in bed and stared into Aramis's eyes. "And am I doomed to spend the rest of my life in this cell?" he asked.

"It appears so," Aramis replied. "Unless you do something about it."

"I don't know why I've been put here, but my enemy must be great and powerful to keep me locked away for my entire life," the young man said.

"He is, and you have been brought here because you pose a great danger to him," Aramis said.

"I suspected as much. I don't think I was always meant to be locked up," the young man replied. "My tutor and nurse took care to raise me as a well-rounded nobleman. Why would they do so only to put me in a cell? But then one morning shortly after I turned fifteen, I was dozing in the summer sun—"

"That was eight years ago?" Aramis interrupted.

"More or less," the young man replied. "I've lost track of time. That fateful morning, I heard my tutor calling for my nurse. He was frantic. I overheard them, you see, and learned that they had lost a letter. My nurse, Perronnette, called it the queen's latest letter. After searching the garden for some time, I saw them look into our well. Then, Perronnette became even more upset. She said the wind had carried the queen's letter into the well, and now it was gone forever. I suddenly realized that the woman who visited us regularly, who brought these letters, must be the queen herself. Perronnette told my tutor that the queen had gone through great trouble and danger to hand-deliver each one. She was sure to be punished for losing it."

Aramis nodded again, then asked, "Do you know what was in the letter?"

"From what Perronnette told my tutor, I learned that the letter contained 'specific instructions about Phillip.' Phillip is my name, you see, so naturally I was curious. As soon as my tutor and Perronnette left the garden, I hurried to the well and climbed down. I found the letter sinking slowly, and was able to retrieve it. Then I crept back to my room. The water had faded the writing, but I managed to read it, anyway."

"And what did you read?"

"Enough to learn that I must have been special, since the queen wanted me looked after. She was trying to find a way to have me taken away from France so the king would never find me."

"What happened next?" Aramis asked.

"Foolishly, I caught a chill from my dip in the well. As I lay in bed recovering for the next few days, my tutor found the letter under my pillow."

"Ah!" said Aramis. "Now I understand how you ended up here."

"I'm not sure exactly what followed," the young man said. "My nurse must have written to the queen to tell her what happened."

"After which, you were arrested and dragged off here, to the Bastille," Aramis said. "When the queen learned that you had seen her letter, she probably thought you had also discovered the great secret she so desperately wanted to protect. She must have panicked and sent you here."

The young man nodded.

"And here you have remained. That is how powerful her secret is," Aramis said. "Now I will tell *you* a secret. One that is thought to be dead and buried."

"I'm listening," Phillip said.

"Years ago, the queen gave birth to a son. When the king heard the news, he rejoiced and ran to tell everyone in the castle. But the queen had actually had *two* sons—twins. When the king learned about the second child, he was not at all happy. He demanded that the news be kept secret. He worried that the second son might try to fight the older one for the kingdom. After all, the difference in their ages was only a matter of minutes. And so the queen's younger son was shamefully separated from his brother and hidden away. He vanished so thoroughly and so quickly that almost no one ever knew he existed. Those who did know were sworn to secrecy."

"His mother abandoned him," the young man said quietly.

"Here is a portrait of the son who grew up to become King Louis XIV," Aramis said, handing the young man a small, realistic painting the size of his palm. Then he gave him a mirror.

Aramis allowed Phillip some time to gather his thoughts and to compare the portrait with the image in the mirror.

"I'm doomed," the young man said at last. "He is my exact double—my twin. The king will never allow me to be seen."

"I wonder, who is the real king? The man in the portrait, or the man in the mirror?" Aramis asked.

"The king is the man who sits on the throne right now," the young man said sadly. "Not the man in prison. Royalty is power, and as you can see, I am powerless."

"Now, sir, listen carefully. The king could be the man who leaves prison—who sits on the throne where his friends place him."

"Don't tempt me," Phillip said. "You give me a glimpse of ultimate power, but I can still hear the jailer's footsteps in the corridor. Get me out of here, and I may begin to believe you."

"Those are my intentions, Your Highness," Aramis said. I don't believe your brother has been a good leader to our people. He is immature, deceitful, and suspicious, and I fear he will lead us into an unnecessary war."

"And what will happen to my brother if you succeed?"

"You will decide his fate when you are the king."

With that, Aramis stood and kissed the prisoner's hand, as if he were already the king.

"When I see you again, I will say, 'Good day, sire,'" Aramis said.

"Until then, no more dreams, no more shocks in my life," the young man replied, placing his pale fingers over his heart.

CHAPTER 2

Three Friends and a Tailor

ᴄ∽

D'Artagnan was worried about Porthos. The Musketeer hadn't heard from his friend in weeks, so he decided to pay him a visit. When he arrived, he found Porthos sitting on the edge of his bed. He was looking sadly at a pile of suits that were strewn across the floor in a mess of fringes, braids, fancy embroideries, and clashing colors.

"Ah," Porthos said when he saw D'Artagnan. "It's you! *You'll* give me an idea."

Porthos stood with some difficulty, his old knees cracking, and crossed the room to hug

D'Artagnan with an affection that seemed to renew his strength.

"You're always welcome, my dear friend," Porthos said. "But today you're more welcome than ever."

"Are you down in the dumps?" D'Artagnan asked.

"I received an invitation to the celebration Mr. Fouquet is throwing at Vaux," Porthos replied.

"But the king said that only his closest friends will be at that party," D'Artagnan said. "You've been invited? Congratulations! What could *possibly* have you so sad?"

"I've nothing to wear," Porthos said, and sighed.

D'Artagnan was dumbfounded. "Why, you've got over fifty suits on the floor," he said.

"Fifty, yes, and not a single one fits me!" Porthos replied.

"How is that possible?" D'Artagnan asked.

Mousqueton, Porthos's assistant, cleared his throat. He had been waiting at the door.

"Unfortunately, I have gained weight," Mousqueton said.

"Why should your waistline affect the fit of Porthos's suits?" D'Artagnan asked.

"Let me explain," Porthos answered. "I hate getting measured. It's too personal, standing there while a stranger pokes and prods and pushes you around. Years ago, I noticed that Mousqueton was my size, so I sent him to be measured for suits in my place. Our system worked quite well, until Mousqueton's easy life here began to get the better of him. As you know, I try to keep myself dressed in the most fashionable suits, and I never keep my old ones. Well, by the time Mousqueton was measured for this recent batch of suits, he had grown fatter than I am, and now none of my suits fit. And I don't have any of my old ones left."

"I suppose Mousqueton will enjoy his gift of fifty new and quite fashionable suits," D'Artagnan said, smiling.

"Very funny," Porthos said. "But I'm still at a loss. I only received my invitation yesterday, and there's no good tailor who can make me a proper suit in time for the party the day after tomorrow. And Aramis told me to arrive a day early, heaven knows why."

"Aramis?"

"He's the one who invited me," Porthos said. "Ah, when I think that I have no suit for the party, I want to smash something."

"Don't smash anything, my powerful friend," D'Artagnan replied. "Have you tried the tailor, Mr. Percerin?"

"Who is he?"

"Why, he's the king's own tailor, you fool," D'Artagnan said. "He's probably busy, but I'm sure he'll do this for me."

"The king gets measured, too?" Porthos asked.

"He likes to look stylish, just like you," D'Artagnan said, and laughed.

Mr. Percerin was close to eighty years old, and lived in a grand mansion. When D'Artagnan and Porthos arrived, they saw hundreds of people gathered out front, waiting for their time with the tailor. D'Artagnan approached the guards and said, "I'm here on the king's business," and they allowed him and Porthos to enter immediately.

The old man was working in his studio, draping some gold-colored fabric over a dress-maker's dummy. Catching sight of D'Artagnan, he approached him, not happy, but still polite.

"Mr. D'Artagnan," said Percerin. "Please excuse me, but I'm very busy."

"Yes, I know. You're working on suits for the king to wear at Vaux. I'm sure they'll be the most beautiful in the world," D'Artagnan said.

"Five suits, and they *will* be beautiful, but first they must be made," Percerin said.

"Bah, you still have two days. Look here, I've brought you a new client," said D'Artagnan. "My friend Porthos is a close friend of Mr. Fouquet, the man who owns the castle at Vaux, where the grand celebration is to be held. The suit you make for Porthos is to be worn at that very same party."

"Aha, I see," said the tailor. "I would like to make you a suit, sir, but there simply isn't enough time."

Then a new voice spoke up from the doorway.

"Don't say that, sir, especially when I'm the one asking you."

At the sound of that gentle voice, D'Artagnan turned. It was Aramis.

"Hello, dear friends," Aramis said. "Come, Mr. Percerin, make this suit for my friend Porthos, and I guarantee that you will also please Mr. Fouquet."

Aramis had more even influence on Mr. Percerin than D'Artagnan did, for the tailor merely nodded, turned to Porthos, and said, "Get your measurements taken on the other side of the room."

Porthos left, feeling enormously pleased and important, and D'Artagnan went to talk with Aramis.

"If you're as free as I am, Aramis, perhaps we can talk and catch up," D'Artagnan said.

"No, I wanted—"

"Ah, you have something private to say to Mr. Percerin?" D'Artagnan asked.

"Yes, but not private from you," Aramis said. Aramis was working on his plan to free the king's twin brother, and he did not want to arouse his friend's suspicions by keeping secrets. "Mr. Fouquet and I have hired a painter to create a portrait of the king, but we want to show the king wearing one of the new suits Mr. Percerin is making for him."

"But only I know how the suits will look, or even which fabrics I will use," said Percerin.

"That is precisely what I'm asking you to reveal to me," Aramis said.

The tailor was so surprised by this request that he could only giggle at first.

"It may seem like an odd thing to ask," Aramis said, "but I have no choice. You see, Mr. Fouquet wants to give the king the greatest surprise possible. A wonderful portrait is one thing, but to show one of the new suits in the portrait, before the king has even seen it himself, that will show a level of thought and planning that is sure to please his highness. I have no intention of forcing you to show me the suits you're making, but Mr. Fouquet did say that if he could not have the portrait done as he wants, he would be forced to tell the king how you spoiled his gift."

"I would never interfere with Mr. Fouquet's wish to please the king," Percerin said, stammering.

He took out several partially constructed suits from a side room, and told Aramis to call in the painter. Then the tailor described how they would look when completed. When no one was watching, Aramis slipped a sample of the fabric into his pocket.

CHAPTER 3

Aramis Returns to the Bastille

The huge clock on the Bastille struck seven in the evening. Tonight Aramis was the warden's guest. The two men were having a friendly dinner together. Midway through the meal, the warden's assistant arrived with an envelope — an order from the king that had just been delivered. Aramis had known the letter was coming, so he pretended to drink from his glass and watched the warden read. Suddenly the warden laughed.

"The king's office says they're in a rush to release a prisoner tonight," he said, and laughed again. "They grab a man one day, feed him for years, and warn you to watch out for him. Then, when you've grown used to treating him as a dangerous person, they tell you to set him free and add 'Rush' to their request. Doesn't that seem crazy to you?"

"And will you release the poor man tonight?" Aramis asked.

"Ah, I'll release him first thing in the morning."

"My friend, I may have been a soldier once, but now I'm a priest. Charity drives me to encourage you to obey the order immediately. This poor man has suffered long enough. You just told me he's been here several years. His moment has come. Set him free, I beg you."

"Just like that? In the middle of supper?" the warden asked. "Very well, I'll do it. But our meal will grow cold."

The warden walked to the door to speak to one of the guards outside, and left the letter lying

on the table. Alone in the room, Aramis took a nearly identical letter from his pocket and switched it with the one on the table.

"It's impossible," the warden said when he returned. "I can't release him."

"Why not?" Aramis asked, trying to control his nervousness.

"It's the middle of the night, and he doesn't know Paris anymore. How can I just let him go now? It would be like releasing a blind man into a den of lions."

"I've got a carriage," Aramis said. "I'll take him wherever he wants to go."

"You have an answer for everything," the warden said, and called for a guard to come into the room. "Have Mr. Seldon released from his cell and brought to the front gate."

"Seldon?" Aramis asked.

"That's the name of the man being released."

"Don't you mean Marchialli?" Aramis asked.

"No, the letter said to release Seldon," the warden replied.

"I saw the name 'Marchialli' written in large letters," Aramis said, reaching across the table and picking up the letter. "Look, it says so right here."

"Amazing," the warden said. "I'm certain I saw the name 'Seldon' written there a few minutes ago. I even remember a small blot of ink below his name. This letter has no such mark."

"Well, whatever you may have seen, this order says to release Marchialli," Aramis said.

"This Marchialli is the same prisoner you visited so secretly the other day," the warden said.

Aramis said nothing. Instead, he continued eating what was left of his dinner.

"Perhaps I should send a messenger to confirm this order," the warden said. "I must make no mistakes."

"Does the king's signature not appear in this letter?" Aramis asked.

"It does, but it can be forged."

"Very well," Aramis said. "I can see that you are a man who respects the orders given by his superiors. You are also a very careful man. Give me a pen and a blank piece of paper."

When Aramis had them, he wrote, *I guarantee that the order brought to the warden is valid and must be carried out immediately.*

He signed it, *By order of the Bishop of Vannes.*

The warden's hands trembled as he took the letter from Aramis. Finally he sat in a chair, as if exhausted.

"Very well. I must do as you say, for you are,

after all, the bishop. I have my suspicions, and it appears to me that you're playing me for a fool, but it also appears that I have no choice. How should I proceed?" the warden asked.

"How do you normally release an inmate? Just follow your regulations," Aramis said.

The warden went to speak with his guard again, leaving Aramis alone in the room. Within half an hour, Aramis heard a door closing in the courtyard. A few minutes later, the warden returned, followed by the prisoner.

Before they left, Aramis asked the warden, "Does my personal order pose a problem for you?"

"I think you've done something strange tonight," the warden said. "Something that I don't want to know about. If I get in trouble, I want your letter at hand."

Aramis agreed to the warden's request, for he wanted to leave as quickly as possible with the prisoner. Then he and Phillip silently sped away in the carriage.

Once they were far from the Bastille, Aramis called to his driver and told him to stop.

"Before we go any farther, we need to talk, Your Highness," Aramis told the prisoner. "The best place for it is here, in the middle of the forest. No one else will see or hear us."

"I'm listening," the young man said.

"I have pulled you up from darkness and I will elevate you to the highest position on earth. You are the son of King Louis XIII and the brother of King Louis XIV. You are the rightful heir to the throne of France, and tomorrow or the day after, you will sit on that throne. You and your brother are absolutely identical. If you behave as he does, no one will even know that you have taken his place. There is no danger as long as your boldness is as strong as your resemblance to the king."

"You're forgetting our consciences, which

could cry out," the young man said. "And there is remorse, which could tear us apart."

"True," said Aramis. "There is weakness of the heart. But I haven't told you everything I have to say. I can see that you're hurt, sick, almost wiped out from your experiences. More than anything, I want you to be happy. I have another offer for you."

"Speak," Phillip said, with an alertness that caught Aramis's attention.

"I know of a small, peaceful town in the countryside, where a man could spend his life as a fisherman. I can give you enough money to buy up a large section of land there. You could take the money and live in freedom."

"Before I make up my mind," Phillip said, "let me think by myself. I need to be surrounded by the sounds of the outdoors, of freedom."

"As you please," Aramis said, bowing respectfully.

The young man left the carriage, his body trembling as he took a few unsteady steps. For the first time in years, the young man was free. He breathed in the warm air of the countryside and heaved a sigh of joy.

These moments were dreadful for Aramis. He worried his plan was about to fall apart because he hadn't considered the effect of some leaves and a few puffs of fresh air on the human body. Phillip's sad eyes kept gazing at the sky, as if looking for an answer.

Finally, he bowed his head. His thoughts came back to earth, his eyes hardened, and his forehead creased. He approached Aramis quickly and grabbed his arm.

"Let's go!" he said. "Let's go to where we'll find the crown of France. That's my decision!"

Aramis bowed.

"Let me ask Your Royal Highness an important question," Aramis said. "I had a notebook smuggled to you containing information about the people in your court, along with instructions to memorize this information. Have you done it?"

"Ask me anything!" Phillip said. "My mother is Anne of Austria. I know of Miss Valliere, who is in love with the king."

"Be careful with her," Aramis cautioned. "She loves King Louis very much and she will be hard to trick. Do you know your ministers?"

"There's Mr. Colbert, a gloomy, ugly man, who is the minister of commerce, and Mr. Fouquet, the superintendent of finance. The two are political enemies."

"There's one other person who will be watching you closely. Someone who could cause us trouble," Aramis said.

"You mean D'Artagnan, the captain of the Musketeers," said Phillip.

"He is one of my dearest friends, and I will tell him everything in due time, but be careful. He's a man of action, and he is loyal to the king, even though he disagrees with him and even dislikes him at times."

Phillip nodded. "I know about your other friends as well, Porthos and Athos. And Athos's son, Raoul. I know he loved Miss Valliere, until the king stole her away.

"As for Mr. Fouquet," Phillip continued, "what shall I do with him?"

"Make him the minister of commerce for the kingdom," Aramis said. "He will replace Colbert."

"And I will make you my prime minister."

"Not right away," said Aramis. "That would be too astonishing for people. It would be better if I first was named the new cardinal of France."

"I will appoint you cardinal immediately," Phillip said. "You can ask for more, anything you like."

"There *is* something else I hope for," Aramis said. "Since you will be a strong and powerful king, and you will extend France's power, *my* power should extend beyond the church in this country, too."

"I know what you want," the young man said. "I will make you the cardinal of France first—the head of the French church. Then you will become my prime minister. And finally, you will tell me what I must do to have you elected pope, the ruler of the church worldwide."

"You have read my thoughts," said Aramis. "For many years now, ever since I stopped being a Musketeer and rededicated myself to the church, that has been my ambition. I believe that together we will be a force for good in the world. I only hope I haven't blinded myself with ambition."

CHAPTER 4

Getting Ready for the Party

The only problem with Mr. Fouquet's castle at Vaux was that it was *too* magnificent. It would make even a king feel jealous. Fouquet oversaw the arrangements for the party and, exhausted, he went back down the steps, where he spotted Aramis.

Fouquet joined his friend, and the two men walked over to a large, nearly completed painting. The artist was covered with sweat, splattered with several different colors, and pale with fatigue and inspiration. He rapidly threw on the final touches with his brush. It was the portrait of the king in his new suit.

As the two men admired the artist's work, they heard the sentinels announce the arrival of the king at a town just a few miles away.

"Imagine, there are some people who wonder why we have such royal festivities," Aramis said.

"I'm not like most people and I wonder the same thing," Fouquet said.

"You should be smiling. This is a day of joy," Aramis said. "People use these parties to make the king happy and to show how much they respect him, and your party will outdo any other."

"Believe it or not," Fouquet replied, "the king doesn't like me at all, and I don't care much for him. But you know, the closer he gets to my castle, the more special I feel. After all, he *is* still the king, and he's coming to *my* castle for a celebration I'm throwing in his honor."

Aramis didn't answer. Instead, he smiled and said he was leaving to change his clothes for the party.

"Which room are you in?" Fouquet asked.

"In the blue chamber on the third floor," Aramis replied.

"That's the room directly above the king," Fouquet said. "You'll have to be careful not to move around or make any noise at night, or you'll upset him."

"I'm a quiet man, and I've only brought one assistant," Aramis said as he walked away, thinking of Phillip, who was hiding in his room.

Meanwhile, D'Artagnan was puzzling over his chat with Aramis at the tailor's mansion. He wondered why Aramis had asked to see Percerin's designs for the king's new suits.

He had a perfectly sensible explanation, but I know my old friend. I can tell when he's up to something, D'Artagnan thought.

He was used to the political games people played at court—everyone always plotting against one another. In fact, D'Artagnan had recently learned that Colbert was planning something against Fouquet. But Fouquet wasn't helping his own situation, either. This party was terribly expensive, and he was already under suspicion of handling the king's money badly.

D'Artagnan thought about talking over his suspicions with Mr. Colbert, but he was afraid he might reveal something about Aramis by mistake. The Musketeers' old oath, "All for one, and one for all," rang in his memory, and D'Artagnan decided to confront his old friend directly when he saw him.

King Louis arrived at the gates of Vaux at seven o'clock in the evening. Fouquet had been waiting at the gate for half an hour, smiling and nervous but also happy to get his enormous party underway.

At first the king was cheerful in the magnificent castle, but he soon began to feel irritated. He thought about his own castle and its luxury, which seemed cheap compared with Fouquet's home. For dinner, they ate from gold dishes that had been made especially for Fouquet by the finest artists. The same level of quality and art could be found in all the furniture and details throughout the castle. The entire place swarmed noiselessly with people. Everything had been arranged to flow together and move smoothly. Although this angered King Louis, it delighted the other visitors, who showed their admiration with awed silence and attention.

CHAPTER 5

The Plot Against Mr. Fouquet

D'Artagnan wasted no time in finding out where Aramis was staying. When he reached his friend's room, he was happy to find that Porthos was there, too. Except Porthos didn't budge. Having eaten a lot at dinner, he had actually dozed off in his chair. His snoring was constant and deep, and D'Artagnan and Aramis had to speak over it.

"Do you like it here?" Aramis asked D'Artagnan.

"I like it very much, and I also like Mr. Fouquet."

"You know, I've heard rumors that the king doesn't like him, and was even going to have him put in jail. But now it seems the king has changed his opinion," Aramis said.

"Yes, in fact you've just reminded me of something I thought of over dinner," D'Artagnan said. "It occurred to me that the real king of France is not Louis XIV."

"What!?" cried Aramis, his eyes locking with D'Artagnan's. Aramis wondered if D'Artagnan had learned of his secret plan.

"In some ways, the real king is Mr. Fouquet," said D'Artagnan. "After all, Fouquet has his hands on all the money. Just look at this castle, this party. It must have been very expensive. It could make Fouquet appear to have even more power than the king."

"I assume Mr. Colbert gave you that idea," Aramis said. "Have you noticed how much Colbert dislikes Fouquet?"

"It's easy to see," D'Artagnan said.

"Well, this party will probably cost Fouquet his entire fortune. But if King Louis thinks Fouquet has spent everything just to make him happy, that will make Fouquet look good."

"It's all just so crazy," D'Artagnan said. "Like that portrait."

"What portrait?"

"The one that's going to be a surprise for the king. That's why you asked Mr. Percerin to show you those samples of cloth, isn't it?" D'Artagnan asked, and paused to measure his friend's reaction. He didn't know what to expect, but his instincts had been telling him that Aramis was up to something.

"It's merely a matter of courtesy," Aramis replied.

"Do you trust my instincts?" D'Artagnan asked. "You used to, in the past. Well, now my instincts tell me that you're carrying out a secret project."

"D'Artagnan, if I had a project that needed you, I'd have told you by now," Aramis said.

"Look at us," D'Artagnan said. "There are three of the old four here in this room. You're deceiving me, I'm suspicious of you, and Porthos is asleep. A fine trio of friends, aren't we?"

"I can tell you only one thing," Aramis said.

"My friendship is as strong as ever. If I have to keep secrets from you, it's because of others and not because of you."

"I fear that you're conspiring against the king."

"If that were true, would you help me?" Aramis asked.

"I would do more than that. I would save you," said D'Artagnan. "Such an act would be treason, and I would try to stop you — to protect you from punishment."

"You've got all your guards and Musketeers here," Aramis said. "What could I possibly do to the king?"

The seriousness of Aramis's words gave D'Artagnan complete satisfaction, and he thanked Aramis.

At that, Aramis turned his face toward a dark corner of the room. He was ashamed that he had deceived D'Artagnan.

"Are you leaving?" Aramis asked, turning

to embrace D'Artagnan and trying to hide his embarrassment.

"Yes, I must get back to the room next to the king's chamber. I'm supervising the guards."

"Well then, take Porthos with you! He snores like a cannon," Aramis said. "I don't know where he's staying, but I can't have him here. This is my room and I need to sleep."

D'Artagnan slapped Porthos on the shoulder, and the big man let out a roaring yawn.

"D'Artagnan, old friend!" Porthos said. "What are you doing here? Oh right, I'm at Vaux for the party, aren't I?"

Aramis saw them out with a gentle chuckle. Once they were gone, he quickly bolted the door, drew the curtains, and called out for Phillip, who emerged from an alcove in the corner of the room.

"Mr. D'Artagnan is quite suspicious," Phillip said.

"He's devoted to protecting the king," Aramis said. "Even if he doesn't care for your brother, D'Artagnan will risk his life to protect him."

"I thought so," Phillip said. "What do we do now?"

"You're going to observe the king closely so you can see what he does before bed. I'm going to slide back a part of this floor, and you'll be able to watch the king's room through the opening," Aramis said.

After Aramis made all the preparations, he asked Phillip what he saw.

"I see the king," Phillip said, and shuddered as if encountering an enemy. "He's talking to a man sitting at his side. I believe it's Mr. Colbert."

Downstairs, Louis said, "Tell me, where does Fouquet get the money for these things?"

"I believe this will give you an idea," Colbert said, handing him a letter. "Sometimes the dead still speak to us."

"It's written by the late cardinal Mazarin," the king said, reading the document. "This says thirteen million francs were given to Fouquet some years ago, when Mazarin was still alive. I didn't know about that."

"The accounts don't show that money, which means Fouquet must have kept it for himself," said Colbert. "With that kind of money, a man could certainly build a castle as great as this one."

The king lowered his head, but he didn't answer Colbert.

Aramis and Phillip were shocked.

"If I were the king, I would not respond to this right away," Phillip said. "I would think it over until tomorrow morning."

In the room below, the king finally looked up and saw Colbert waiting impatiently for a reply. The king quickly changed the subject. "I see it's getting late, Mr. Colbert. I'm going to bed."

"Ah, I see. In that case I will—"

"Wait until tomorrow. I'll make a decision by morning," the king said.

"Very well," Colbert said, but it was clear that he was beside himself with impatience.

The real festivities began the next day, with banquets and performances and strolls around the beautiful gardens and courtyard of the castle. Throughout the day, King Louis stayed reserved and quiet. In the evening, he went for a walk alone in the park, where Colbert and Miss Valliere found him.

Miss Valliere had seen the king's scowling face and blazing eyes, and she could read his emotions clearly. She realized his anger was aimed at someone. Colbert moved a respectful distance away while Louis motioned for her to advance.

"My dear," the king said, taking her hand,

"may I ask what's wrong? You look like you're about to cry."

"If I am sad, sire, it is because you are sad," she said.

"Oh, you are mistaken. It's not sadness I feel. It's humiliation," Louis said. "Wherever I am, no one else should be the master, but look around and you'll see that Mr. Fouquet has outdone me. And when I think that this man is a disloyal servant who makes himself grand with money he has stolen from me—"

"Your Majesty!" Miss Valliere said.

"What, my dear? Are you going to take Mr. Fouquet's side?"

"No, sire. I only wonder if you've received the correct information about him," she said. "He is a good man. Your Majesty knows how many false accusations happen in the court."

The king signaled for Colbert to approach and told him to inform Miss Valliere of Fouquet's crime. The story of Fouquet's thievery shocked her.

"And now, Colbert, go tell Mr. D'Artagnan that I have orders for him," Louis said angrily.

"Mr. D'Artagnan!" cried Miss Valliere. "Why do you need him? I beg you to tell me."

"Why, to arrest that arrogant Fouquet!" the king said.

"In his own home?" she asked.

"Why not? He's just as guilty here as he is anywhere else," Louis replied.

"But Mr. Fouquet is ruining himself, going broke just to honor you with this party," she said.

"Are you actually defending this traitor?"

"I'm not defending him, sire. I'm defending you," she said. "Even if Mr. Fouquet is guilty, he is still an important man because the king is his guest. You honor his home by coming here, and a man's home is a sanctuary where he should be safe."

Miss Valliere lapsed into silence. The king couldn't help but admire her. Colbert could see that his plans had been crushed for now. The king drew a long breath, shook his head, and took Miss Valliere's hand once again.

"Why do you speak against me?" he asked. "Do you know what that scoundrel will do if I give him a chance to catch his breath?"

"He is like a small animal to you, one you can catch anytime you like," she replied.

Finally Louis nodded, submitting to the passion of her voice, and agreed not to arrest Fouquet just yet. Colbert was furious, but then his face brightened with an idea. He rummaged through his briefcase, removing a sheet of paper that was folded like a letter. The document was slightly yellow, but it must have been quite precious because it made Colbert smile just to look at it. Then his hateful eyes focused on the couple in the shade, the girl and the king, who were about to be discovered by an approaching group of people. It wouldn't be proper for the king to be seen talking so closely with a woman to whom he wasn't married.

"Leave me," the king said to Miss Valliere. "The rest of the royal party is coming."

She hurried away and vanished among the trees.

"Ah! Miss Valliere has dropped something," Colbert said, pretending to pick up the document he had removed from his briefcase. "It's a letter. Here it is, sire."

The king took the letter just as the group arrived. As soon as Fouquet led the king back to the castle, a mass of flames as dazzling as dawn burst from behind the castle with a blinding roar and lit up the tiniest details of the gardens. Amid the fireworks, the king read the letter, which he had assumed was a love letter Miss Valliere had written to him. As he read, his face turned red.

His muffled anger would have terrified anyone who could see into the king's heart. He was filled with jealousy and rage, and a keen grief twisted his heart.

The letter had been written by Fouquet several years earlier, when he had been trying to win the heart of Miss Valliere. Colbert's spies had learned of Fouquet's affection and tracked down the letter among Miss Valliere's belongings. The young woman had been in love with Athos's son, Raoul, at the time, and had politely turned Fouquet away. Not long afterward, she had fallen in love with King Louis and left poor Raoul stricken with grief, much like the king now felt.

Fouquet saw the anger in the king's face, but was unaware of its cause. Colbert saw the king's fury and delighted in the gathering storm.

"What's wrong, sire?" asked Fouquet. "You seem to be suffering."

"I *am* suffering, but it's nothing," the king

replied. And without waiting for the fireworks to end, he returned to the castle. After Fouquet bid him good night, Louis said, "You'll be hearing from me soon. Please send in Mr. D'Artagnan."

Aramis and Phillip were in their room above, eavesdropping as attentively as ever.

"How many soldiers do you have here?" King Louis asked when D'Artagnan arrived.

"I have the Musketeers," said D'Artagnan, surprised by the suddenness of the king's question. "And I have twenty guards, and thirteen other soldiers."

"How many would it take to arrest Mr. Fouquet?" the king asked.

D'Artagnan stepped back and nearly gasped.

"Are you going to tell me it's impossible?" Louis yelled with a cold, hateful fury.

"I never say anything's impossible," D'Artagnan said.

"Then do it!"

D'Artagnan turned and walked to the door. Then he stopped and said, "Excuse me, sire, but I would like a written order to make this arrest."

"Why? When is the king's word not enough for you?"

"When a king's word is spoken in anger, it may change when the anger lessens," D'Artagnan replied. "Once you've gotten over your anger, you'll feel bad about this. At that point, I would like to show you your written order. It won't change anything, but the regret you will feel will at least prove that it's wrong for a king to lose his temper."

"It's wrong?" the king cried. "You served my father and his father. Did they never lose their temper?"

"They did, but only in private," D'Artagnan said.

"The king is the master everywhere," the king said. "I can do as I please."

"If I may speak bluntly, sire," D'Artagnan interrupted, "that is the kind of nonsense people say to make you feel good. You probably heard that from Mr. Colbert, and it is simply not true. The king becomes the master of someone else's home only when he has disgraced himself by pushing the true owner out."

The king bit his lip.

"This man has ruined himself to please you," D'Artagnan said. "And now you want to arrest him! It is an insult to your kingdom to behave like this. You ask if I have enough soldiers— ridiculous! Mr. Fouquet lives only to serve you. He would not put up a fight unless you asked him to."

"Very well," Louis grumbled. "Do not arrest him in public. Guard him until tomorrow. Then I will give my final decision. Now leave me alone."

CHAPTER 6

Kidnapping the King

༄

The king's fury lost strength in the nighttime, settling eventually into a painful weariness that crushed him into a deep sleep. In his dreams, the king saw the ceiling of his room shift and move away. Then he felt his bed move. Finally he noticed that the paintings, curtains, and furniture were all gone, replaced by a dull gray that thickened more and more into a shadow. After a minute that dragged by like a century, the bed reached an area of black and icy air, and then it stopped. The king saw the light of his room as if he were looking up from the bottom of a well.

This is a horrible dream, he thought. *It's time I woke up! Come on now, wake up!*

Suddenly Louis realized that not only was he already awake, but his eyes were open as well. To his right and left stood two armed men, each wearing a vast cloak with a hood so the king couldn't see their faces. One man was holding a small lantern. They had been carrying him, and now stood him up on the moist floor. He asked the lantern holder, "What's going on? What kind of joke is this?"

"It's no joke," said one of the men in a hollow voice. It was Aramis. The bishop had disguised his voice so the king wouldn't recognize him.

"Are you working for Fouquet?" asked the bewildered king.

"It doesn't matter whom we're working for,"

said the man. "We are your masters, and that's that."

The second masked man was a tall hulk. He stood as straight and motionless as a block of marble. This was Porthos, but the king didn't recognize him, either.

"Answer me!" the king yelled, stamping his foot.

"We will *not* answer you, my little man," the giant boomed. "There's no reason to answer you, except to say that you are indeed a nuisance."

"Just what is it you want?" cried Louis, angrily crossing his arms.

"You'll know soon enough," replied the lantern holder.

"I won't budge!" Louis cried.

"If you resist, my young friend," said the larger of the two men, "I'll pick you up and roll you in my coat."

The king was terrified. After a few moments of thought, he shook his head and sighed.

"I guess I've fallen into the hands of two assassins," he said. "Let's go, then."

Neither man responded. The three men marched through a long, winding passage until they arrived at an iron door, which the lantern holder unlocked. The king hesitated, and the large man pushed him through. Louis realized he was standing outdoors.

"I repeat," he said, shocked at being handled so roughly, "what are you planning for the king of France?"

"Try to forget that phrase," replied the lantern holder. "You are not the king."

The men walked through the darkness, surrounded by trees, until they came to a carriage. Louis and the lantern holder climbed inside. The larger guard closed the door and locked it from the outside, then climbed into the driver's seat and hurried the two horses off along a path. They rode fast for several hours, until they reached the outskirts of Paris. At the gates of the Bastille, Porthos shouted, "By order of the king!" to the guard, who let them pass immediately. When they finally stopped in the courtyard, the driver yelled, "Wake the warden!"

Ten minutes later, the warden appeared at the front door. The driver unlocked and opened the carriage door, then grabbed a large musket and pointed it at the prisoner's chest. "If he opens his mouth, shoot him!" Aramis muttered.

"Fine," said the other man calmly.

The lantern holder approached the warden and lowered his hood. Before the warden could speak, Aramis whispered, "Let's go inside."

"What brings you here in the middle of the night?"

"A mistake, my dear warden," Aramis said. "Apparently, you were right the other evening."

"About what?" the warden asked.

"Why, about that prisoner you released, my friend," Aramis said. "You remember? We thought the letter was for a man named Marchialli."

"Yes, but you forget," the warden said. "I had doubts and didn't want to release him. It was you who forced me to."

"Oh, that is too harsh a word," Aramis said. "I merely recommended it."

"Yet you still took him away with you."

"Well, my dear warden, I was wrong. And I've brought you a royal order to release the correct man. You remember? His name was Seldon," said Aramis, handing him the order. It was the one he had stolen from the warden's table during his last visit.

"But this is the same order," the warden said. "I've seen this one before! I recognize this blob of ink in the corner."

"I don't know if it's the same order, but at any

rate, I'm bringing it to you," Aramis said. "And here is Marchialli back. Return him to his cell immediately and we will try to forget about this mistake."

"But I need another order to take him in!" the warden cried.

"Don't talk such nonsense, my friend. You sound like a child. Where is the order you received when I was last here, the one to release Marchialli?" Aramis asked.

The warden hurried to his office, and Aramis followed. Inside, he opened his desk and produced the document. Aramis took it and held it over a candle's flame until it was completely destroyed.

"What are you doing?" the warden asked in sheer terror.

"I've simplified everything, my friend," Aramis said, and smiled. "Now you no longer have the mistaken order for Marchialli's release. And I've even brought him back. It's as if he never left."

The warden wrung his hands.

"From a friend like you, I can keep no secrets," Aramis said, and led the warden back outside. Then he whispered, "You can see the resemblance between this poor man and—"

"And the king, yes," the warden interrupted.

"Well, guess what he tried to do with his newfound freedom?"

"How should I know?" the warden asked.

"He tried to pass himself off as King Louis," Aramis said. "He dressed as him and even tried to enter the palace. Of course, he was discovered right away. He's clearly insane."

"What should I do with him?"

"Don't let him talk to anyone. You see, when the king learned of this insanity, he was furious," Aramis said. "He ordered that anyone who lets this man communicate with someone other than me will be sent to the dungeons! No one, not even the king, is to see him. Do you understand?"

"I do," the warden said.

The warden escorted them back to the prison cell. Porthos kept the musket pointed at Louis the entire time. He still wore his hood, and Aramis put his hood back on before Louis could see his face. The king entered the cell without saying a word. He was pale and exhausted.

"He really does look like the king," the warden murmured to Aramis, "but less than you say."

"So you wouldn't have been fooled?" Aramis asked.

"Of course not! Anyone can see that he isn't actually the king, once you really look at him."

After leaving the cell, and bidding the warden good-bye, Aramis and Porthos took the carriage and sped from the prison. Meanwhile, the king felt stunned and shattered. He leaned against the wall of his cell and closed his eyes.

"I can't be dead or dreaming," he said out

loud. "They kidnapped me in my sleep, the scoundrels! Me, a prisoner!"

All at once, the chill of the room dropped like a cloak on Louis's shoulders.

"How can I be locked up?" he asked himself, reassured to hear his own voice. "Mr. Fouquet must be plotting against me. I was drawn into a trap at Vaux. But what can they be thinking? The world will know I'm missing. There must be a warden here. He'll listen to me."

Louis cried out, but no one responded. He grabbed his chair and banged it against the heavy door. It made a terrible noise that echoed throughout the tower, but still, no one answered. Then he ran to the window and began calling through the bars. Still no response.

The king's blood boiled with anger. He was used to being in command. His body trembled with fury at this betrayal. He smashed the chair and used the pieces to batter the door for hours until he was exhausted.

"Hey! Are you crazy?" snapped the guard on the other side of the cell's door.

"Sir, are you the warden of the Bastille?" Louis asked.

"My good man, your mind is unhinged," the guard replied. "Now shut up!"

The guard walked away, ignoring Louis, who continued to call after him. Two hours later, Louis no longer felt like a king. In fact, he barely felt like a human being. Instead, he felt like a madman, scratching at the door, trying to pull up the floorboards, and shrieking so dreadfully that the old Bastille seemed to tremble.

As for the warden, he never even stirred. The guard told him about the prisoner, but the warden thought, *Why bother going to see him? This place is full of madmen.*

CHAPTER 7

The Plans at Vaux

⤳

Fouquet was about to go to bed when D'Artagnan knocked on his door. Fouquet answered, and D'Artagnan walked inside with his hand on his sword. He didn't say a word. Instead, he merely looked at Fouquet and motioned for him to sit down.

"I'm not arresting you tonight," D'Artagnan began, "but the king has ordered me to stay here and guard you."

"And what about tomorrow?" Fouquet asked, turning pale.

"Well, you never know what tomorrow will bring," said D'Artagnan.

With an air of surrender, Fouquet sat down on the edge of his bed.

Meanwhile, young Phillip had crept downstairs. Alone in the king's chamber, he felt a sudden rush of emotion racing through his heart and couldn't sleep. His ears perked up at every sound. His heart fluttered with every scare. Toward morning, someone—more shadow than body— slipped into the royal chamber. It was Aramis.

"Well?" Phillip asked.

"Everything is done," Aramis replied.

"And Mr. Porthos?"

"As far as he knows, he was rescuing his king from an impostor," Aramis said.

"How should I reward him?" Phillip asked.

"Make him a duke," Aramis said, and smiled. "He will enjoy it tremendously."

At that moment, Aramis heard something in the hallway.

"It's daylight. I believe your brother made an appointment to meet someone here," he said.

"Yes, Mr. D'Artagnan," said Phillip. "It must be him!"

"Now, be very careful," Aramis warned. "He knows nothing of what we've done. He has seen nothing and is far from suspecting anything, but it's too soon for you to be alone with him."

D'Artagnan knocked on the door. He was exhausted. He had been awake all night keeping watch over Fouquet. In fact, he had just left the man's room after making him promise to stay put. He knew Fouquet was a man of honor and wouldn't try to escape.

When Aramis opened the door to the king's room, D'Artagnan was so surprised, he nearly cried out.

"You're here," the Musketeer stammered.

"His Majesty asks that you tell anyone wishing to see him that he is still resting from last night," Aramis said.

"Ah," D'Artagnan said, but he was still in a state of shock. Why was Aramis speaking for the king?

"And as far as Mr. Fouquet is concerned, the king no longer wishes you to guard him."

D'Artagnan nodded and started to walk away when Aramis called to him.

"I'll go with you," he said. "I want to see Mr. Fouquet's delight at the news."

CHAPTER 8

The King's Unexpected Friend

⌒

"I see you've brought me Mr. Aramis," Fouquet said to D'Artagnan when the Musketeers arrived.

"And something even better," D'Artagnan said. "Freedom, by order of King Louis! You can thank Aramis here. He's the one who convinced the king to change his mind."

As Aramis had expected, Mr. Fouquet was overwhelmed with joy.

D'Artagnan turned to Aramis and said, "Could you possibly do something for me? Tell me: How have you managed to become the king's closest adviser when you and he haven't spoken more than a few words to each other in your life?"

"I can't hide anything from a friend like you," Aramis said. "The truth is, the king and I have met hundreds of times, but it was always in secret."

Aramis ignored the redness that colored D'Artagnan's face at the news, and turned to Mr. Fouquet, who was just as surprised as the Musketeer.

"Sir," said Aramis, "the king is your friend now more than ever. He has been moved to the depths of his heart by the beautiful celebration that you have so generously offered him."

D'Artagnan saw that these two men had something more to say to each other. He obeyed his instinct to be courteous and left them to discuss their business.

"My dear Aramis, my bishop," said Fouquet, locking the door. "I think it's time you explained what's going on."

"You should really ask why the king was going to have you arrested in the first place," Aramis said. "Do you remember the late cardinal Mazarin and how much he hated you?"

"Of course. I caught him trying to steal millions from the king," Fouquet said.

"It appears he left a letter making it look like he had given you thirteen million francs, which of course aren't in the accounts," Aramis said. "You were declared a thief."

"My God!" Fouquet cried.

"That's not all. Do you remember the letter you wrote to Miss Valliere some time ago?"

"Unfortunately, I do," Fouquet said. "That was a mistake. I know now that she never cared for me."

"Well the king has that letter. He thinks you wrote it recently, which gave him even more reason to hate you," Aramis said.

"Then why did he pardon me?"

"The king has given me no instructions concerning you," Aramis said.

"But I don't understand!" Fouquet cried.

Aramis collected his thoughts for a moment. Then he told Fouquet the story of the king's twin brother, Phillip, who had been hidden away for years.

"Is it possible?" cried Fouquet, clasping his hands. "Who else knows?"

"His mother knows, of course," Aramis said. "The king, my friend's brother, knows nothing."

"I see where you're going," Fouquet said. "You knew this secret and threatened to reveal it unless the king pardoned me."

"That isn't it at all," Aramis said. "I forgot to mention one important fact about these brothers.

They are absolutely identical. No one can tell them apart, not even their mother. The same noble features, the same movements, the same voice."

"But what about their minds?" Fouquet cried. "Their intelligence, their knowledge of life?"

"Oh, that is where the resemblance ends. The prisoner in the Bastille is far superior to his brother. And were that poor victim to leave prison and take over the throne, France would know a leader with more powerful virtue and noble character than ever before," Aramis said.

For a moment, Fouquet buried his face in his hands, crushed by the immense secret he had just been told. Then his head snapped up, his face pale and twisted.

"I understand!" he said. "You're asking me to join in your conspiracy. You want me to help you substitute the imprisoned son of Louis XIV for the son now sleeping in the royal chamber."

Aramis smiled at the thought that this plan had already happened. "Exactly."

"But it doesn't seem to have dawned on you that this political action could turn the whole kingdom topsy-turvy," Fouquet replied after a painful silence. "You must realize we would have to assemble all the nobility, the politicians, the church. We would have to convince them to dethrone the king and reveal the scandal of his and his brother's lives. And once we finish, if we could even get that far——"

"I don't understand you," Aramis snapped coldly. "Now, if there has been any chaos, scandal, or even great effort——any at all——in substituting the prisoner for the king, I challenge you to prove it."

"What?" Fouquet cried, whiter than the handkerchief he was using to mop his forehead.

"Go to the king's chamber," Aramis went on calmly. "I challenge you to prove that the prisoner from the Bastille has replaced his brother."

"But the king," stammered Fouquet, terror-stricken by the news.

"Which king?" asked Aramis. "The king who hates you, or the king who loves you?"

"Yesterday's . . . king?"

"He's in the Bastille. He's taken the place his brother occupied for too long," Aramis said.

"Good heavens! And who took him there?"

"I did, and in the simplest way," Aramis said. "I kidnapped him last night. While he descended into darkness, the other king rose into the light. I don't believe there was a single sound. Lightning without thunder never bothers anyone."

Fouquet let out a dull cry, as if struck by an invisible blow, and buried his face in his rigid fingers. "You did that?" he murmured.

"I did it quite well, if I say so myself. And what do you think?" Aramis asked.

"You've dethroned the king? You've imprisoned him? And it happened here, in Vaux, in my home?" Fouquet asked, moving as if he wanted to pounce on Aramis. But he held back. "That crime was committed in my own home!"

"Crime?" said Aramis, stunned.

"That horrible crime!" Fouquet continued, growing more and more angry. "A crime worse than assassination. A crime that will dishonor my name and condemn my family to be hated forever!"

"You're delirious," Aramis said in a shaky voice. "Be quiet, be careful!"

"He was my guest. He was my king!" Fouquet yelled.

Aramis stood, his eyes bloodshot and his mouth quivering.

"Have you lost your mind?" Aramis said. "Am I dealing with a lunatic?"

"You're dealing with a man of honor! A man who will prevent you from carrying out your crime. A man who would rather die, who would rather kill you, than let you dishonor him and his family," Fouquet said.

For a moment, Fouquet looked toward his sword, which was hanging by the door. Aramis looked at it, too, and looked back at Fouquet with an expression that warned him against moving to take it. Then Aramis raised his head, and a shimmer of hope returned to his eyes.

"Mr. Fouquet," he said, "think about everything lying ahead for us. Justice has been done.

The king is still alive, and his imprisonment has saved your life."

"You may have been acting in my best interest," Fouquet said, "but I refuse to accept your services. You will leave this castle immediately. You are my guest, and you will not be hurt here. I will allow you to escape."

"Escape," said Aramis, sneering as if he could not believe what he was hearing.

"You have my word. No one will follow you for at least four hours. That will give you a head start on anyone the king sends after you. I own the castle on the island of Belle-Isle, and I am giving it to you now as an asylum. You tried to help me, and I will repay you by allowing you to hide there until my soldiers can help you escape to another country."

"Ah," Aramis murmured.

"Leave now, Bishop. As long as I live, not a hair on your head will be harmed while you are on Belle-Isle. Let's both hurry, you to save your life, I to save my honor."

Aramis took two steps back and cursed at the man he had made the mistake of trusting. Then both men dashed from the room and hurried down the staircase that led to the courtyard. Fouquet sent for his best horses, while Aramis ran to Porthos's room.

I'm doomed, Aramis thought. *Once the king knows what I have done, he will figure out that the large man who helped me kidnap him was Porthos. My friend will suffer, too, if he stays. He will have to follow my destiny. He must!*

But Porthos was still sleeping. Aramis entered his room and placed his nervous hand on the giant's shoulder.

"Wake up!" he cried. "Wake up, Porthos!"

Porthos obeyed, stood, and opened his eyes before he was fully awake.

"We're leaving," said Aramis.

"Ah," said Porthos.

"We're leaving on horseback. We must gallop faster than we've ever galloped before."

"Ah," repeated Porthos.

Aramis helped his friend get dressed. As he did so, a noise from the doorway caught his attention. He turned and saw D'Artagnan watching him.

"What are you so nervous about?" D'Artagnan asked.

"We're about to leave on a secret mission," Aramis said.

"Lucky you," D'Artagnan said with a smile. "You always seem to have some sort of secret mission going on."

"Have you seen Mr. Fouquet?" Aramis asked.

"Just now, as he was getting into his carriage," D'Artagnan said. "He had enough time to say good-bye to me, and then he was off. Why do you ask?"

"Listen," said Aramis, hugging D'Artagnan. "Your time has come again. I predict that my actions today will double your importance to the king."

Aramis said good-bye to D'Artagnan, and he and Porthos ran to the stables, where they mounted two horses and rode away. D'Artagnan watched until they disappeared into the distance.

On any other occasion, D'Artagnan thought, *I would say those two are escaping from something. But these days, politics are so strange that an escape is called a mission.*

He laughed to himself and returned to his room.

Hours later, when Fouquet arrived at the Bastille, he asked if the warden had seen Aramis, and the warden said yes. Fouquet glared at him and said, "Aren't you horrified by the crime you've helped him commit?"

"Nonsense!" the warden said. "What crime?"

"There isn't time to explain, but it's enough to have you locked away in a dungeon for the rest of your life, if you're lucky! For now, take me to the prisoner," Fouquet demanded.

"Who? Marchialli?"

"Who?" Fouquet asked.

"The prisoner Aramis brought here last night," the warden said.

"So that's the name he was given," Fouquet mused.

"He's been an awful annoyance all day, yelling and screaming like a madman," said the warden. "I will need an order signed by the king or by Mr. Aramis to let you see him."

Fouquet was irritated.

"Show me the warrant Aramis used to have him put in jail," he said.

The warden showed him the release warrant for the man named Seldon.

"This is not for Marchialli," Fouquet said.

"But Marchialli hasn't been released," said the warden. "He's still here."

"You said Aramis took Marchialli away and brought him back!"

"I never said that," the warden stammered, remembering how Aramis had destroyed the forged release document.

"You said it a moment ago!" Fouquet yelled.

"It was a slip of the tongue," the warden said. "Listen, I follow the rules. Mr. Aramis brought me an order to release Seldon, and that's what I did."

"I'm telling you the man you call 'Marchialli' has left the Bastille," Fouquet said.

"You'll have to prove that," the warden said nervously.

"If you don't let me see him, I will leave and return with every soldier in France. I will have the Bastille burned to the ground, and I will see that you are arrested and punished for the rest of your life!"

"Stop!" the warden cried. "I don't know what this is all about. I don't know whose orders to follow anymore. If the king judges me, at least I'll finally know who was right and who was wrong in this horrible mess. Very well, let's go see Marchialli."

As they climbed the stairs of the tower, Fouquet heard muffled cries and horrible screaming. "What's that?" he asked.

"That's your Marchialli," said the warden. "That's how lunatics howl."

Outside the door to the cell, Fouquet took the key from the warden and told him to leave.

"Take all the guards with you," Fouquet said. "If anyone approaches before I call, you will take the place of the most wretched prisoner in the Bastille!"

The prisoner's cries grew more and more dreadful. After making sure that no one was nearby, Fouquet began to unlock the door.

"Help me! I'm the king! Help me!" the prisoner screamed. "It was Mr. Fouquet who did this to me! I'm the king!"

The words broke Fouquet's heart. Finally, he opened the door. The two men stared at each other.

"Have you come to finish me off?" Louis asked. His clothes were tattered, his shirt torn and open, his hair wild, and his skin covered with dirt.

Fouquet was so saddened to see the king like this, he almost started to cry. But when he tried to embrace the king, Louis threatened to hit him with part of the chair he had broken earlier that day.

"Your Majesty," Fouquet said in a trembling voice, "don't you recognize your friend? How you must be suffering. Come with me—you are free."

"Free?" Louis said with hatred. "You would set me free after doing all this?"

"You can't believe I'm behind this," Fouquet said. And he quickly explained the entire incident to the king.

"It's a lie!" the king interrupted. "I have no twin!"

"Sire, that man must look at least a little like you or else Aramis would not have planned to have him impersonate you," Fouquet said.

"Very well, then. I will assemble all of my soldiers and we will storm your castle at Vaux!" the king said. "We will capture all of the scoundrels who did this to me, including that impostor who claims to be my brother."

"Your Majesty, to honor the friendship that I once had with Mr. Aramis and Mr. Porthos, I have given them asylum on Belle-Isle."

The king was furious. His eyes flashed with hatred, and Fouquet felt sure he was doomed. But he knew he had done the honorable thing.

CHAPTER 9

Twins and Old Friends

Back at Vaux, the new king was playing his role correctly, following his morning ritual exactly as he had watched his brother do it the previous day. Wearing one of the suits that Aramis had secretly had constructed from the sample cloth from Mr. Percerin's mansion, Phillip watched everyone enter his royal chamber.

He shivered at the sight of his mother. Thinking about how she had sacrificed him for the good of the kingdom, and how much that must have pained her, filled his heart with sorrow.

He promised himself he would try to love her and would not punish her. She spoke to him as if he were the king. Clearly, no one could see that he was not Louis.

"I heard a rumor that Mr. Fouquet was on your bad side," his mother said. "Is that true?"

"He was accused of theft," Phillip said. "But he is a man of honor. Fortunately, I learned that the claim was false before I took any action."

His mother seemed a little confused by this, but she didn't challenge his decision.

As the morning went on, with discussions of politics and plans, everyone—family, officers, assistants—recognized Phillip as the king. He had the right manners, voice, and habits. But he was growing impatient to see Aramis, and Fouquet's absence worried him.

Hours passed, and then, during a conversation with his mother and Mr. D'Artagnan, Phillip heard a commotion outside.

"That's Mr. Fouquet's voice," D'Artagnan said.

"Aramis can't be far off, then," Phillip added with relief.

But then he saw something that he had never expected to see so closely. King Louis stood at the door, staring furiously at Phillip from across the room. Behind Louis, Fouquet appeared.

The queen was holding Phillip's hand. When she saw Louis, she wailed, as if seeing a ghost, and dropped her son's hand. Everyone in the room looked from one brother to the other. There were several moments of stunned silence. Each of the brothers stood with fists clenched, trembling in fury. They sized each other up as enemies, and each seemed ready to pounce on the other. On top of their astounding physical resemblance, they were wearing the exact same suit.

Louis had not expected an obstacle like this, so he thought he would be recognized the instant he entered the room. He had never known of Phillip's existence. As the king, he could not endure the thought of anyone being his equal. He was terrified at the sight of his twin brother.

Fouquet was amazed. He realized Aramis had been correct about his twin's perfect resemblance. He had been convinced that Aramis was either lying, or that the false king was not Louis's equal. Fouquet felt like a fool. Each brother had a right to the throne, and he should have stayed away from meddling in politics of the highest order. This situation was beyond him.

D'Artagnan stood with his back to the wall and stared at the scene before him. He knew in his heart that Aramis was somehow responsible for this, and he feared for his friend's life.

Suddenly Louis rushed to the window and pulled the curtain back, filling the room with sunlight. "Mother, don't you recognize your own son?" he cried.

Then Phillip said calmly, "Mother, don't you recognize your own son?"

Louis ran to D'Artagnan and said, "Musketeer, help me! Look at our faces and see who is paler. He has spent years in prison, away from the sun. See how white his skin is compared with mine? Look!"

D'Artagnan seemed to wake up from his daze, and began to think logically. *He's right,* D'Artagnan thought. *That one does have the sickly complexion of a man who's been in jail for too long.* D'Artagnan shook his head and placed his hand on Phillip's shoulder. "Sir, you are under arrest," he said.

Phillip couldn't move. He stared at his brother. In his eyes, he blamed Louis for all his past misery and all his future punishment. Louis understood everything he saw in his brother's gaze and he could not say anything in return. Instead, he led the rest of his family out of the room. Before his mother left, Phillip said to her, "I would have cursed my mother for having made me so

unhappy, but having met you for even a short time, I can't do it."

D'Artagnan shivered when he heard Phillip's noble words. Then Phillip asked about Aramis.

"So long as I am alive and free, no one will harm him," Fouquet said.

Phillip turned to him. "You're Mr. Fouquet. I'm glad to finally meet you."

Fouquet bowed, and the three men continued into the courtyard. Once there, Colbert called to D'Artagnan and gave him a letter. The Musketeer read it, then crumpled it furiously.

"What is it?" Phillip asked.

"An order from the king," said D'Artagnan.

Fouquet recovered the document and unfolded it. After he read it, he showed it to Phillip, who read, "Mr. D'Artagnan is to bring the prisoner to the island prison of Saint-Marguerite. There, he is to cover the prisoner's face with an iron mask, which is never to be removed."

"I understand," Phillip said. "I'm ready."

"Aramis was right," Fouquet whispered to D'Artagnan. "This one is just as noble and kingly as the other. He did deserve to be king."

"Even more than his brother," D'Artagnan agreed.

Many miles away, Aramis and Porthos were taking advantage of the head start Fouquet had given them, and were speeding across the countryside.

Porthos still believed the king was going to make him a duke. Aramis could not bear to tell his friend he had gotten them both in deep trouble, and that they were running for the lives.

On their way to Belle-Isle, they passed through a part of the country that Aramis recognized as Athos's home. Aramis dearly wished to see their old friend from the Musketeer days in this time of trouble. As he and Porthos rode toward Athos's mansion, Porthos said, "I understand."

"What do you understand, my friend?" Aramis asked.

"The king is sending us to work with Athos on a secret project," Porthos said. "All we need is D'Artagnan and we'll be as strong a force as we were in the past!"

"Go ahead and keep guessing," Aramis said.

Athos and his son, Raoul, had been staying in this part of the country ever since Raoul's love affair with Miss Valliere had ended. They were discussing how Raoul could get over his sadness—which was their usual topic of discussion over dinner—when Aramis and Porthos knocked on the front door.

Raoul let out a joyful cry when he saw the two men, and gave Porthos a hug. Aramis and Athos embraced like old friends.

"My friend, we won't be staying long," Aramis said.

"Long enough to tell you of my good luck, though," Porthos said. "The king is going to make me a duke! As a reward for a secret mission Aramis and I carried out last night," he added.

While Porthos and Raoul laughed, Athos noticed that Aramis remained gloomy. Aramis took Athos by the arm and asked the others to give them a moment of privacy.

"My dear Athos," he said, when they were alone, "I'm grief-stricken. I've plotted against the king. The conspiracy failed, and they're probably hunting for me now. The worst of it is that I involved dear Porthos in my plot. He committed himself to helping me without knowing any details. You know how loyal he is, and now he is as doomed as I am."

"My God!" Athos said, and he glanced at Porthos, who smiled at them from across the room.

"You are one of my dearest friends, and I want you to understand why I did this," Aramis continued, and he told Athos the entire story. By the end of it, even Athos was pale and nervous.

"It was a grand idea," Athos said. "But it was also a grand mistake. It's a crime, my friend."

"Success was so certain," Aramis said.

"But you misunderstood the character of Mr. Fouquet. He is an honest and honorable man, even if it means his own downfall," Athos said.

"And I'm a fool for having such bad judgment," Aramis said. "Now I'm escaping with poor Porthos.

The king will never believe he was innocent. He will pay for my mistake. I don't want that to happen. We're heading to Belle-Isle. Fouquet's men can hold off many of the king's soldiers from there. After that, a boat will take us out to sea, perhaps to England or Spain. I know many people in each country who could help us. Once there, I'll find a way to make up with King Louis and get Porthos back into his good graces."

"You have gained a lot of power since we last spoke," Athos said, smiling.

"Can you ever forgive me for what I've done?"

"I know you wanted to defend the weak, unfairly treated brother," Athos said. "I might have done the same thing. I'll give you and Porthos my best horses to ride to Belle-Isle."

Athos bowed and shook Aramis's hand. Then he walked to Porthos and hugged him.

"I was born lucky, wasn't I?" a joyful Porthos murmured.

CHAPTER 10

Departures and Arrests

ↄ

A few hours after Aramis and Porthos left, the Duke of Beaufort arrived for dinner with Athos and Raoul.

"I've actually come to make my farewell," the duke said as they sat at the dinner table. "After fifty years here and many bizarre adventures, I've decided to take up one last challenge. I've been asked to lead an army regiment in Africa!"

"Africa," Athos repeated. "That's very far from here, and I expect it will be a dangerous mission."

"It's madness for me to take up this adventure

so late in my life, but I couldn't resist testing myself once more," the duke said. Then, turning to Raoul, he added, "In fact, I was thinking you might want to come with me. I know you've suffered a terrible heartbreak, and this would give you something to dedicate yourself to with all your heart and soul."

Athos turned pale at the words. Before he could think of a way to discourage his son, he saw Raoul's eyes light up.

"I was hoping you would ask me that," Raoul said. "I heard of your upcoming adventure from some of my friends, who are soldiers in your regiment. When I heard, I wished I could go. It's so far away and so dangerous. It would take me away from all my sadness."

"You wish to leave me?" Athos asked.

"Not at all," Raoul said, turning red. "How can you believe that? I love you, Father."

"He knows what he wants," the duke said.

"What is he going to do here other than rot away with grief? The navy offers him a wonderful future."

Raoul smiled so sadly, it broke Athos's heart. Athos knew his son wanted to leap headfirst into danger just to forget his lost love. He worried that Raoul would act foolishly, mistaking his eagerness for bravery, and would get himself hurt or killed in battle.

"Sir, I would be glad to serve on your ship," Raoul said. "However, I'll be doing it to serve you and my country, not the king, for as a person he is still my enemy and the cause of my pain."

After the duke left, Athos and Raoul sat in silence. Both men kept their emotions hidden deep in their hearts, yet each sensed the pain and anxiety the other felt. Finally, Athos stood to go to bed and Raoul hugged him. Then Athos said in a shaky voice, "Soon you'll have left me, my son!"

"I had already made up my mind to run away,"

Raoul said. "If I don't leave here, I'll die of pain and love. Send me away before you see me like that."

"Then you're planning to get yourself killed in battle?" Athos asked. "Just tell me."

"You are the only thing that I live for," Raoul said. "I owe you everything, and will do all I can to come back to you."

Tenderly hugging his son, Athos said, "You've spoken like a man of honor. You are free to do what you want, Raoul."

∽

Over the next few days, Raoul made plans to lead part of the duke's regiment. Athos and Raoul agreed to sail to Antibes, where they would meet with the duke and the entire force, and where father and son would part.

While helping Raoul gather the necessary supplies, Athos met up with D'Artagnan's former servant, Planchet, who owned a store in Paris. Planchet told Athos that D'Artagnan had gone off on another secret mission. He even showed Athos a map that D'Artagnan had made several marks on.

Athos was concerned for his friends. Aramis and Porthos were running from the king, and D'Artagnan, the king's top soldier, was off on a secret mission. Luckily, it appeared from the map that D'Artagnan was not headed toward Belle-Isle, where Aramis and Porthos were hiding. Instead, the island of Saint-Marguerite was circled in red.

Athos wanted to consult with D'Artagnan about how he could help Aramis and Porthos, so he and Raoul hired a boat to take them to Saint-Marguerite. It was a detour, but they had time before they were to meet with the duke.

It was a beautiful little island. The governor of the region kept his garden there. Fig trees, orange trees, and more luscious gardens filled the land.

For a while, Athos and Raoul walked along the garden's fences without finding anyone. Then they spotted a soldier carrying a basket of food toward the fortress.

Athos heard someone call out from a little tower in the prison. He looked up and saw something white and shining in the frame of a barred window. It was a plate of some kind. A loud hissing sound moved toward the ground, and Raoul hurried over to the moat that surrounded the prison and picked up the plate. The hand that had tossed it waved to the men from the barred window and then disappeared.

A message had been scratched on the plate: *I am the brother of the French king. I am a prisoner here.*

The plate dropped from Athos's hands while his son tried to understand what those words meant. At that same instant, a shout came from the dungeon and a musket barrel appeared on

the crest of the wall. Swift as lightning, Athos and Raoul lowered their heads and hid in the tall grass. There was a shot, and the bullet hit a stone nearby. They heard soldiers gathering and running in their direction.

Athos and Raoul looked at each other. Without saying a word, each drew his sword and prepared to do battle. They were about to charge toward the soldiers when a familiar voice shouted from behind them, "Athos! Raoul!"

"D'Artagnan!" the two men replied.

"Lower your guns!" D'Artagnan yelled at the soldiers, then ran to meet his friends.

"What's happening here?" Athos asked. "Were they going to shoot us?"

"I might have killed you myself," D'Artagnan said, hugging each of them. "Luckily, I recognized you. Ah, my friends, how fortunate!"

"But, why were you going to shoot us?" Athos said.

"You picked up something the prisoner threw down," D'Artagnan said. "The king has ordered me to stay here with the prisoner and kill anyone who tries to communicate with him."

When he read the plate that Raoul handed him, D'Artagnan turned pale.

"So it's true?" Athos asked.

"Hush!" D'Artagnan whispered. "The governor is on the island. He's on his way over here now. If he thinks you read this, even I could not protect you from being punished. King Louis has given the harshest orders regarding this prisoner. Listen to me now. You are from Spain! You don't speak or read French. Do you understand?"

The governor was approaching. "What's going on?" he hollered. "Why aren't you arresting those men?"

"I was right," D'Artagnan replied. "I met these men in Spain last year. They don't speak a word of French."

While he spoke, he quickly scratched out the message on the plate with the handle of his sword. The governor arrived and asked why D'Artagnan had destroyed the message.

"You know the king's orders," D'Artagnan said. "This was a message from the prisoner, and no one is to communicate with him."

"But these two men read it," the governor said.

"They can't read a word of French," D'Artagnan said. "Let them be."

The governor nodded and insisted that Athos and Raoul join him at the fortress for dinner. D'Artagnan agreed, although he would rather have seen his friends a hundred miles away. Once alone, Athos asked D'Artagnan what was going on.

"It's simple," D'Artagnan said. "I've brought a prisoner here whom the king will not allow anyone to see. When you arrived, the prisoner tossed you a message. The governor and the other soldiers saw you pick it up. That prisoner is crazy. You can't believe what he wrote."

"Perhaps we should ask Aramis about that," Athos said coldly.

"You've seen him?" D'Artagnan cried.

"He came to me as a fugitive. He told me enough to believe what your prisoner scrawled onto his plate," Athos said. "Don't worry, you know how good I am at keeping secrets."

"You've never held a secret as dangerous as this one," D'Artagnan said. "Everyone who comes in contact with it gets into trouble."

Over dinner with the governor, Athos and Raoul kept up their act. They pretended to speak only Spanish and used D'Artagnan as their translator. Later, D'Artagnan led his friends into one of the gardens, where the prisoner was being taken for a walk. The man was dressed in black and had a guard on each side. Except for holes for his eyes, nose, mouth, and ears, his head was completely encased in a visor and helmet of polished iron. A storm was brewing, and the clouds reflected on his horrible mask.

"That is an unhappy man," D'Artagnan murmured to his friends.

When they returned to the fortress, a message had arrived by boat for D'Artagnan. He read it and shouted for joy.

"My time here is over," he said to Athos and Raoul. "The king has ordered me back to Paris."

"So you're leaving us?" Athos said sadly.

"Yes, but we'll meet again, that is for certain," D'Artagnan said.

That night, the three friends took a boat from Saint-Marguerite. When they landed, D'Artagnan bid farewell to Athos and Raoul.

The next day, Athos and Raoul completed the last leg of their journey together and arrived at the port where the duke's ships were waiting. Father and son spoke for hours about their lives and their love for each other. Neither wanted their final moment to come, but it did at last. They shook hands, and then embraced. As the boat pulled away with Raoul on it, Athos could only wave from the shore. Then he sat, feeling abandoned and grief-stricken. He remained there, watching Raoul's ship sail away until it vanished in the distance.

Back in Paris, D'Artagnan was learning about many things that had happened while he was guarding poor Phillip. Colbert had succeeded in turning the king's opinion against Mr. Fouquet.

Even though Fouquet had rescued King Louis from the Bastille, the king was once again considering arresting him. Poor Fouquet was slowly being driven mad from the pressure and the endless waiting for the final order to arrest him.

Finally, Fouquet met with the king, Colbert, and D'Artagnan. Fouquet was feeling sick from all the pressure, and asked that he be allowed to leave the king's castle and return to Vaux.

"If I'm not under arrest, that is," he said.

"Of course you aren't," the king said. "Why would you think such a thing? Perhaps Mr. D'Artagnan could ride with you back to your home, especially since you're feeling ill."

Fouquet declined the offer as politely as he could, and left immediately. Shortly after, the king told D'Artagnan, "I want you to follow Fouquet. Once he's away from my castle and someplace where there won't be a commotion, I want you to arrest him. Lock him up in a carriage with steel plates over the windows so he won't be able to communicate with anyone."

"That will take days to build," D'Artagnan said.

"It has already been made by Mr. Colbert," the king said. "It is waiting for you outside, along with new horses."

Satisfied, the king left the two men. When they were alone, Colbert handed D'Artagnan a letter with further orders. After arresting Fouquet, D'Artagnan was to take a fleet of soldiers to Belle-Isle and capture Aramis and Porthos.

"I know you have friends there," Colbert said. "Your orders are to arrest them or destroy the fortress completely."

CHAPTER 11

An Unusual Reunion

At the far end of the pier at Belle-Isle, which was being lashed by the furious evening tide, Aramis and Porthos were having a long and animated conversation.

"Let's sit here on the rocks," Porthos said. "Sit and explain this to me so I can understand it. Explain to me what we are doing here."

"Porthos . . ." Aramis said awkwardly.

"I know that a false king wanted to dethrone the real one," Porthos said. "And I know that we are on a mission. What I don't understand is why no one has come with supplies, or more soldiers, or instructions for us. All we've done is wait, and you won't tell me anything."

Aramis stood, and Porthos grabbed his arm. "I'll tell you what I think," Porthos said. "I imagine something bad has happened back in Paris."

"Porthos! What's that?" Aramis interrupted, pointing to a black dot on the water. "Two boats! No, five!"

"I see seven," Porthos said. "No, an entire fleet! They're sending us reinforcements!"

Instead of answering, Aramis buried his head in his hands. Then he cried, "Porthos, sound the alarm! Have the cannons loaded and ready!"

Porthos studied his friend, as if to convince himself that Aramis hadn't lost his mind. "Allow me to try to understand, Aramis. That fleet over there—it's from the king, isn't it?"

"There are two kings of France, Porthos. One

who likes us, and one who doesn't. Which one do you think owns this fleet?" Aramis asked.

Porthos seemed crushed by the question, but he also seemed to have a better idea of the danger he now faced.

"I've got strange things to tell you," Aramis said. "I've lied to you, old friend."

"You lied?" Porthos asked. After a few moments, he added, "Was it for my own good?"

"I thought so, Porthos. I sincerely thought so," Aramis said. "I was helping the man who wanted to dethrone King Louis. We were helping the man who isn't the king, and now we are in a great deal of trouble."

"Ah, I see," Porthos said thoughtfully. "And the promise that I would become a duke?"

"It was made by the man who isn't king," Aramis said. "Please forgive me, Porthos. My crime was my ambition."

"Now that's a word I have always liked," Porthos said. "I can't possibly blame you for that. I have spent much of my life trying to gain more wealth and fame."

After they had prepared the fortress for a battle, they heard the guards calling for them. A small boat was arriving from the fleet. When Aramis and Porthos got to the pier, D'Artagnan called out. "Tell your soldiers to back off so we can talk alone," he said.

"But if the king has sent D'Artagnan after us, why don't we simply tell him that it has all been a mistake and ask him to help us?" Porthos whispered to Aramis.

"Sadly, our old friend probably has orders that would force us to fight him," Aramis said.

"Fight D'Artagnan?" Porthos said. "It would never happen. Never!"

D'Artagnan landed, and the three men went

to find a quiet place to talk. Once they were alone, they hugged one another.

"Well, we are certainly in a bad spot now, aren't we?" D'Artagnan said. "This island has been surrounded by the fleet, and they believe you two are rebels. The king wants you, and he is going to have you."

"Then it's over," Aramis murmured.

"Not if we come up with a plan," D'Artagnan said. "I already have the beginnings of one. If I can keep this from becoming a battle and get you safely aboard my ship, I might be able to smuggle you away."

"You were always the best at finding ways to get us out of danger," Aramis said.

After tenderly hugging his two old friends once more, D'Artagnan left the island and returned to the fleet. When he stepped back onto his ship, he called for all the officers to gather.

"Gentlemen, I've just taken a boat to study the fortress at Belle-Isle," D'Artagnan said. "It will be very difficult for us to take this place by force and arrest everyone. The soldiers here serve Mr. Fouquet. They don't know that he's been arrested, and they would not believe us if we told them, for they are fiercely loyal to him. Therefore, I want to invite the two senior officers from the island to come on board so we can discuss a surrender with them."

The officers looked at one another, and most seemed to agree on this plan. But then one of them produced a sealed letter and handed it to D'Artagnan. It read,

Mr. D'Artagnan will not have meetings with anyone from Belle-Isle. The senior officers on the island are to be arrested and chained in the ship's hold, far away from Mr. D'Artagnan.

King Louis XIV

CHAPTER 12

The Battle on Belle-Isle

D'Artagnan was furious that the king had expected his attempt to save his friends from battle, but he did not despair. His mind raced, and he hit on a new idea.

"Gentlemen," he said to the officers, who were still discussing the king's surprising letter. "It appears that the king has given someone else a secret order, and no longer trusts me to lead this mission. I will therefore go to the king immediately and resign. We must return to France right now so we can see who is truly in charge of the fleet and the Musketeers. Get to your posts!"

Everyone moved to obey his order. *If this works,* D'Artagnan thought, *my friends will be able to escape as soon as the fleet leaves the island.* But another officer produced a sealed letter from the king, which said,

> *If Mr. D'Artagnan tries to resign, he will no longer be in charge of this fleet or this mission. In such a case, no one is to obey any of his orders. He is to return to Paris immediately, without the fleet. If he refuses to leave, he is to be arrested.*
>
> *King Louis XIV*

D'Artagnan went pale. The king had thought of everything. He considered doing battle with the officers, but the room was quickly filling with more soldiers who were not Musketeers, and who would not hesitate to arrest him.

The officers walked D'Artagnan to a small boat, and he was taken away under guard. As they sped away from Belle-Isle, D'Artagnan looked back and heard a cannon fire.

Aramis and Porthos heard the same thing and realized D'Artagnan's plan had failed. They ran outside, where the guards told them boats were coming with more soldiers for a ground attack. Aramis gave the order for the island's soldiers to surrender.

"There's no need for these loyal men to die because of my mistake," he said to Porthos. "But you and I must try to get away. There's a grotto at the far end of the island—a small cave with a tunnel that leads to the water. I had a small boat tied there right after we arrived. If it's still there, we may have a chance to escape!"

"You are a clever man," Porthos said. "The king doesn't have us yet! Let's go underground."

The grotto was so far away that the two friends had to run for hours to reach it. By the time they got there, it was long past midnight. Aramis was loaded down with money, food, and weapons, while Porthos carried two kegs of explosives in his massive arms. Aramis took a lantern and carefully examined every nook and cranny of the cave.

There were three compartments to the grotto, connected by a small corridor that opened up at the water's edge. The boat was still there, rocking wildly in the waves. The two men loaded the ship and were about to push off when they heard soldiers at the entrance to the grotto.

"They've followed us!" Aramis whispered. "And we can't sail yet. I see one of the king's ships out there."

"Back into the cave," Porthos ordered. "They can't see us in there, and it's too small for several soldiers to enter at once. We'll have a good chance to fight them one at a time if we need to."

As Aramis and Porthos crept back to the front of the grotto, they heard the soldiers approach. There must have been fifty or more, led by a group of hounds who had been following the men's trail. The two friends positioned themselves at the entrance to the cave. As each soldier entered, Aramis and Porthos attacked them.

The fight lasted a long time, and more and more soldiers charged into the cavern. Slowly,

Aramis and Porthos were driven farther back into the dark cave, toward the water. During a pause in the action, one of the soldiers called out, "Who are you? Who are we fighting?"

Porthos responded, "The esteemed bishop, Aramis, and his friend, the would-be duke, Porthos!"

A murmur spread through the soldiers at the mention of their names.

"The legendary Musketeers!" repeated the men. "The Musketeers are the men who hold Belle-Isle? We're trying to arrest two heroes!"

The thought that these young soldiers were fighting two of their idols made them shiver, half in excitement, half in terror.

The battle had now moved into the last of the three compartments in the grotto, and soon, Aramis and Porthos would have no more room for retreat. They had held off the soldiers for hours. By now, it was nearly daylight.

"My friend," Aramis said, "I believe more soldiers have arrived. I can hear them."

"Ah," Porthos said calmly. "What should we do?"

"Continuing this fight would be risky. I believe we should allow as many of them to enter this cavern as possible," Aramis said. "Can you get the explosives?"

"I see where you're going," Porthos said.

Porthos lifted the two kegs and brought them to Aramis. They heard the soldiers pushing their way closer, and Aramis put a fuse into each keg.

"Give me the flame," Porthos said. "Then I want you to get to the boat. I will wait until the men are nearly here. Then I'll bring this part of the cave down so they won't be able to reach us."

"I'll help you." Aramis said.

"No. You should go!" Porthos commanded.

Aramis gave a small, burning piece of wood to his friend. They shook hands, and then Aramis ran out to the boat. Now alone, Porthos lit the fuses, which sparked brightly. The soldiers spotted him and began a charge. Then the men in front saw the kegs and understood what was about to happen. There were too many men behind them, and no matter how much they yelled, there was no way to stop the cavern from filling with soldiers. It only took a few seconds. Porthos hurled the kegs at the grotto, then turned and ran toward the rear exit. He dove to the floor and covered his head.

A jet of fire, smoke, and debris churned up from the middle of the cavern, growing bigger as it soared. The walls collapsed. Everything seemed to be burning in a flash that lasted only a moment or two. Then the grotto was silent, filled with sand and dust.

Porthos scrambled to his feet and ran. He spotted the boat a few paces ahead. All at once, the floor moved. The cave was still collapsing, and he only had time to mutter "uh-oh" in surprise before everything crashed around him.

Smoke and rocks burst from the cave, and the boat nearly tipped over from the waves caused by rocks falling into the water. Aramis had to flatten himself to the boat's floor. When it was over, he rowed the boat back, fighting the waves. When the boat neared the cave—or what was left of it—Aramis called out to Porthos.

"Here, here," Porthos said, in a weak voice. "Patience, my friend."

Aramis saw his friend trapped under a large boulder. He leaped ashore and began to pull at the boulder. Slowly, the two men were able to move it, and Porthos crawled free. He was exhausted.

CHAPTER 13

Confrontations at Sea and the Palace

⁓

Aramis, pale and frozen in the chill of dawn, watched the cliffs fade into the horizon as he and Porthos sailed away in their tiny boat. They didn't see any of the king's fleet, and for a short time they felt like they were going to get away. But barely an hour after they hoisted their sail, Aramis saw something in the distance: a white dot that seemed to be moving in their direction.

A few hours later, Aramis woke Porthos and said, "My friend, we're being followed."

He and Porthos tried lowering their sail so

they wouldn't be as visible on the water, but the other ship responded by raising two more small sails to increase its speed. Aramis and Porthos took turns studying the enemy through a telescope.

"It looks like there are twenty-five of them on board," Porthos said. "Brace yourself. I think they're going to fire."

A wisp of smoke appeared over the boat in the distance, and a cannonball hit the water about a mile away from the two friends. It was both a threat and a warning.

"They're going to sink us," Porthos said. "What should we do?"

Even though the situation appeared dire, the old soldiers remained calm and alert. They were still weary from the previous night's battle, but they were ready to continue fighting, if necessary.

"Let's wait for them to arrive," Aramis said. "We should save our strength."

"Agreed. Once we board their ship, we'll have

a chance at fighting them," Porthos said. "It's better than being chased until we're too tired to row anymore."

"Perhaps we have another option," Aramis said thoughtfully.

When the enemy boat reached them, all the men were on deck holding muskets. Two cannons were pointed at the small boat.

"At the first sign of resistance, we shoot!" the skipper of the boat yelled.

With a quick motion, Aramis raised his head, got to his feet, and smiled, his eyes blazing.

"Throw down the ladder, gentlemen," he said, as if he were the commander. The men obeyed.

Seizing the rope, Aramis boarded first. Porthos, meanwhile, took a little longer to climb aboard. To the great surprise of all the sailors, Aramis did not cower. Instead, he walked firmly toward the ship's captain. He made a mysterious and unfamiliar gesture with his hands that only the captain could see. At the sight of it, the captain turned pale, trembled, and bowed his head.

Without uttering a word, Aramis displayed the ring he wore on his left hand to the captain. He looked like an emperor holding out his hand to be kissed. After raising his head for an instant, the officer bowed again with the deepest respect. Then, pointing to his own cabin, he stepped aside and let Aramis pass.

Aramis glanced at Porthos, who wisely remained quiet and followed as if he understood what had just happened. Five minutes later, the captain emerged and ordered the crew to turn the ship toward Spain. While this was being done, Aramis and Porthos returned to the deck and sat down by the railing.

The second in command approached the captain and asked, "Which course are we sailing, sir?"

"Whichever one the bishop here chooses," the captain said.

Aramis whispered to Porthos, "I thought my position as a bishop in the church might still have some power. It was my final hope. I recognized this captain as a high-ranking member of the church, and someone who must obey the orders of a bishop."

"I may have to look into that line of work for myself someday," Porthos said. "Clearly, it has its benefits."

Back at the king's castle, D'Artagnan found that he was being ignored. The king read through some papers, and then carefully put everything away into the drawers of his desk. D'Artagnan remained silent and close to the door. After a few moments, the king said, "Is that Mr. D'Artagnan?"

"It is," replied the Musketeer, drawing closer.

"Well," Louis said, focusing his eyes on

D'Artagnan, "tell me, what did I ask you to do at Belle-Isle?"

"Maybe you should ask that of the endless number of officers who seemed to have an endless number of secret orders from you," D'Artagnan said.

The king lashed out in his response.

"Mr. D'Artagnan, orders were given only to men I judged to be loyal to me."

"I am offended that after all my years of service, a senior officer such as myself should be pushed around and commanded by lesser officers," D'Artagnan shot back. "I am therefore leaving your service. I resign."

"Do you forget that I am your king and that I don't have to explain my actions to anyone?" Louis asked. "You served me badly by siding with my enemies."

"Two former Musketeers who served the king

for years!" D'Artagnan replied. "And you sent an entire fleet after them—it's disgraceful!"

"You are not to judge my actions" the king said.

"I have to judge my friendships, sire. That is why I am leaving your service."

"I had to capture and punish two rebels," Louis said. "Was I supposed to be worried if they were also your friends?"

"It was cruel of you to send me after them knowing that they are among my closest friends in life!"

"It was a way for me to test your loyalty. You failed the test, Mr. D'Artagnan."

"Listen to me, sire. I am a rebellious swordsman when I am told to do wrong. It was wrong of me to pursue those two men. And why not let them escape? Why surround me with spies? Why dishonor me in front of my soldiers?"

"Enough!" Louis shouted. "I am the leader of this kingdom, and I will let no one challenge me on that. You want to spoil my plans and save my enemies? I can destroy you or have nothing further to do with you. But I have an excellent memory, and your service in the past forces me to act mildly. First of all, you are a man of great sense, a man of heart. Second, you have no more reason to be disloyal, for my men have either captured or killed your friends on Belle-Isle."

D'Artagnan went pale.

"Captured or killed!" he cried. "If I thought you were telling me the truth, I would forget all that is good in me and call you a brutal, barbaric man. You don't understand men like Aramis or Porthos, or myself. Captured or killed? I know it could never happen to them."

"Those are the responses of a rebel!" Louis said. "Tell me, sir, who is the king of France, and do you know of any other?"

"Sire," D'Artagnan said coldly, "don't forget that I arrested your twin brother at your request in Vaux. I recognized you as the king before anyone else did."

At these words, Louis lowered his eyes, as if ashamed to remember his dreadful adventure. Almost at the same moment, a messenger arrived and gave the king a letter. Louis read it and turned pale. He remained silent and motionless. Then suddenly he pulled himself together.

"Mr. D'Artagnan, I know you'll learn what I've just been told, so it's better if I tell you myself," he said. "A battle has been fought at Belle-Isle. Over two hundred of my men have been injured, and the rebels have escaped."

D'Artagnan uttered a cry of triumph.

"I want you to understand me," Louis said. "Would you follow a leader who had other kings in the kingdom? How could I accomplish the great things that I have planned? You've known me since my childhood, but now I am grown up. Look around you—all the people bow to me. Bow like them, or choose exile."

D'Artagnan shuddered.

"Perhaps as you look back on these events," the king continued, "you will see that I do have a generous heart. I count on your loyalty and believe in you strongly enough to leave you with the secret of my brother's existence."

D'Artagnan realized that Louis was stronger and smarter than he had thought. The young, inexperienced boy had grown into a strong leader.

"Come, what's holding you back?" the king asked gently. "You've handed in your resignation. Do you want me to refuse to accept it?"

"I am hesitant to take back my resignation. Your work as king will be great—I can sense it. But I've lived through wars and peace. I've served kings and cardinals, and I've been injured more times than I can count. And after all that, I've earned a level of power that allows me to come and go in the king's palace, and to speak to you as I wish. If I stay, I will not be the soldier I was—I will have less power, and I'll miss it. Yet I've done harder things, and I could do it. Not for money, or ambition, or love of the court. If I stay here, it will be because for thirty years I've been in the habit of serving the king, whoever that is, and knowing that I am good at what I do."

D'Artagnan bowed his head.

"My friend," the king said, "you have lost none of your power. I have just grown beyond your control. I will give you back your command, and you will rise to become one of the greatest leaders in my army."

D'Artagnan was deeply moved.

"But what about my friends from Belle-Isle?" he asked.

"Are you asking for mercy on their behalf?" the king asked. "Very well, then. If it means that

I can have my top soldier back, then I will grant it. But things are different now, you must understand. I am no longer a boy. I am the king, and I will not have anyone challenge my authority."

D'Artagnan grasped the king's hand and thanked him. Then, his heart bursting with joy, D'Artagnan dashed from the castle and headed back to Belle-Isle to search for his friends.

Epilogue

ᴄᴏ

It took D'Artagnan several years to find Aramis and Porthos, who had managed to land in Spain and were working for its king. They had many adventures there, but they always missed their friends back in France.

Years later, Aramis and Porthos were named as Spain's official ambassadors to France. They were even invited by King Louis XIV to stay with him. He was older now, and had forgiven them for their actions in Vaux when he was a young man. Back in the palace, they reunited with

D'Artagnan. Athos also made the trip from his remote village in order to see his friends.

The Musketeers sat around the king's table and talked about their many adventures together. There they learned how the king had built an estate for his twin brother on that long-lost island of Saint-Marguerite, and how Phillip had stopped wearing the horrible iron mask years earlier. When the time came to leave, they parted sadly. It was the last time they ever saw one another.

Porthos eventually became a duke in Spain, where he lived for the rest of his life in a lavish castle. Aramis remained a bishop and powerful adviser to the kings of Spain and France. Athos continued his life as a count. Raoul eventually returned from his adventures in Africa, and father and son lived together, the best of friends.

And D'Artagnan continued to lead the king's Musketeers. He eventually became a general in the army, and finally earned the title of field marshal of France—the highest position any soldier could hope to achieve. The day he received the honor, he remembered his three closest friends and the oath they swore to follow: "All for one, and one for all." From that day on, he would say he shared the title of field marshal with three other men.

What Do *You* Think?
Questions for Discussion

Have you ever been around a toddler who keeps asking the question "Why?" Does your teacher call on you in class with questions from your homework? Do your parents ask you questions about your day at the dinner table? We are always surrounded by questions that need a specific response. But is it possible to have a question with no right answer?

The following questions are about the book you just read. But this is not a quiz! They are designed to help you look at the people, places, and events in the story from different angles. These questions do not have specific answers. Instead, they might make you think of the story in a completely new way.

Think carefully about each question and enjoy discovering more about this classic story.

1. Aramis tells Phillip that he risked everything to find him. What is the riskiest thing you've ever done?

2. Why is it so impressive that Porthos was invited to the party at Vaux? What is the best party you've ever attended?

3. Why does Aramis talk to the tailor in front of D'Artagnan? Have you ever kept secrets from a friend or thought someone was keeping secrets from you?

4. Aramis offers to either make Phillip king or to give him money to live in the country. Why do

you suppose Phillip chooses as he does? Which would you prefer?

5. Why does Colbert think Fouquet is stealing the king's money? Have you ever been accused of something you didn't do?

6. Why does Raoul wish to join the Duke's regiment? How does Athos take the news? Have you ever traveled without your parents?

7. D'Artagnan says that Phillip deserved to be king more than Louis. What makes him think that? Who do you think deserves to be king?

8. Where do Aramis and Porthos go to hide from Louis? Where would you go if you needed to hide out?

9. Why do Aramis and Porthos blow up the grotto? Do you think this was brave or foolish? What is the bravest thing you've ever done?

10. Why does D'Artagnan hesitate to take back his resignation? Do you think he makes the right decision? What would you have done in his place?

Afterword
By Arthur Pober, Ed.D.

⁓

First impressions are important.

Whether we are meeting new people, going to new places, or picking up a book unknown to us, first impressions count for a lot. They can lead to warm, lasting memories or can make us shy away from any future encounters.

Can you recall your own first impressions and earliest memories of reading the classics?

Do you remember wading through pages and pages of text to prepare for an exam? Or were you the child who hid under the blanket to read with a flashlight, joining forces with Robin Hood to save Maid Marian? Do you remember only how long it took you to read a lengthy novel such as *Little Women*? Or did you become best friends with the March sisters?

Even for a gifted young reader, getting through long chapters with dense language can easily become overwhelming and can obscure the richness of the story and its characters. Reading an abridged, newly crafted version of a classic novel can be the gentle introduction a child needs to explore the characters and storyline without the frustration of difficult vocabulary and complex themes.

Reading an abridged version of a classic novel gives the young reader a sense of independence and the satisfaction of finishing a "grown-up" book. And when a child is engaged with and inspired by a classic story, the tone is set for further exploration of the story's themes, characters, history, and details. As a child's reading skills advance, the desire to tackle the original, unabridged version of the story will naturally emerge.

If made accessible to young readers, these stories can become invaluable tools for understanding themselves in the context of their families and social environments. This is why the Classic Starts series includes questions that stimulate discussion regarding the impact and social relevance of the characters and stories today. These questions can foster lively conversations between children and their parents or teachers. When we look at the issues, values, and standards of past times in terms of how we live now, we can appreciate literature's classic tales in a very personal and engaging way.

Share your love of reading the classics with a young child, and introduce an imaginary world real enough to last a lifetime.

Dr. Arthur Pober, Ed.D.

Dr. Arthur Pober has spent more than twenty years in the fields of early childhood and gifted education. He is the former principal of one of the world's oldest laboratory schools for gifted youngsters, Hunter College Elementary School, and former Director of Magnet Schools for the Gifted and Talented for more than 25,000 youngsters in New York City.

Dr. Pober is a recognized authority in the areas of media and child protection and is currently the U.S. representative to the European Institute for the Media and European Advertising Standards Alliance.

Explore these wonderful stories in our
Classic Starts™ library.